Note to parents, carers and teachers

Read it yourself is a series of modern stories, favourite characters and traditional tales written in a simple way for children who are learning to read. The books can be read independently or as part of a guided reading session.

Each book is carefully structured to include many high-frequency words vital for first reading. The sentences on each page are supported closely by pictures to help with understanding, and to offer lively details to talk about.

The books are graded into four levels that progressively introduce wider vocabulary and longer stories as a reader's ability and confidence grows.

Ideas for use

- Although your child will now be progressing towards silent, independent reading, let her know that your help and encouragement is always available.

- Developing readers can be concentrating so hard on the words that they sometimes don't fully grasp the meaning of what they're reading. Answering the puzzle questions on pages 46 and 47 will help with understanding.

For more information and advice on Read it yourself and book banding, visit **www.ladybird.com/readityourself**

Book
Band
9

Level 4 is ideal for children who are ready to read longer stories with a wider vocabulary and are eager to start reading independently.

Special features:

Clear type

Full, exciting story

Heidi was happy in the mountains with her grandfather. She liked the trees and flowers and she liked looking after the goats with Peter. Heidi liked the little white goat best of all. Her name was Snowflake.

Richer, more varied vocabulary

14

15

Longer sentences

Heidi was pleased to see Clara, and took her to see all the beautiful things in the mountains.

But Peter was jealous of Heidi's new friend. When no one was looking, he pushed Clara's wheelchair down the mountain.

Detailed illustrations to capture the imagination

40

41

Educational Consultant: Geraldine Taylor
Book Banding Consultant: Kate Ruttle

A catalogue record for this book is available from the British Library

Published by Ladybird Books Ltd
80 Strand, London, WC2R 0RL
A Penguin Company

003

ISBN: 978-0-72327-325-7

Printed in China

Heidi

Illustrated by Tamsin Hinrichsen

Once upon a time, there was a little girl called Heidi.

Heidi lived in a little town in Switzerland with her Aunt Dete. The town was near some mountains.

One day, Aunt Dete said, "Today we will go and see your grandfather. He lives up in the mountains."

As they walked up into the mountains, they saw a boy called Peter. Peter looked after some mountain goats.

Heidi and Aunt Dete walked up to the house where Grandfather lived. Grandfather came out to meet them.

Aunt Dete said, "Heidi, I have to go to Frankfurt. You must stay here with your grandfather."

Heidi was worried. So was her grandfather. He said, "I'm much too old to look after a little girl."

But Aunt Dete went back down the mountain, and Heidi stayed with her grandfather.

"Where will I sleep?" she asked.

Grandfather made her a little bed in the hayloft. Then Peter took Heidi some goats' milk to drink.

Heidi was happy in the mountains with her grandfather. She liked the trees and flowers and she liked looking after the goats with Peter. Heidi liked the little white goat best of all. Her name was Snowflake.

Sometimes, Heidi went to see Peter's grandma, who was blind. Heidi told Peter's grandma about all the beautiful trees and flowers that she saw in the mountains.

But one day, Aunt Dete came back from Frankfurt.

"Heidi," she said, "it's time you went to school."

"Where must I go?" said Heidi.

"To Frankfurt," said Aunt Dete. "I will take you to stay with my friends who live there."

Grandfather was sad.
"Does Heidi have to go?" he said.

Heidi was sad, too. "I want to stay here with Grandfather and Peter," she said.

But Aunt Dete said, "No. You must go to school."

Aunt Dete took Heidi to live
with some of her friends in
a big house in Frankfurt.

A little girl called Clara lived
there. Clara could not walk.
She had to stay in a
wheelchair all the time.

Heidi liked Clara, but she wasn't happy living in Frankfurt. She wanted to go back to Grandfather and Peter in the mountains.

At night, Heidi dreamed that she was in the mountains with Snowflake, the little white goat.

One day, when Heidi came home from school, Clara said, "Last night, the maid saw a ghost on the stairs. Tonight, Daddy will stay up so that he can see the ghost, too."

So that night, Clara's father went to look for the ghost. His friend, the doctor, went with him. As they were looking, there was a noise on the stairs. It was Heidi, walking in her sleep.

"So this is the ghost, after all," said Clara's father.

The doctor took Heidi back to her bedroom.

"What were you dreaming about?" said the doctor.

"I was dreaming of the mountains," said Heidi. "I am happy here, but I miss my grandfather and Peter."

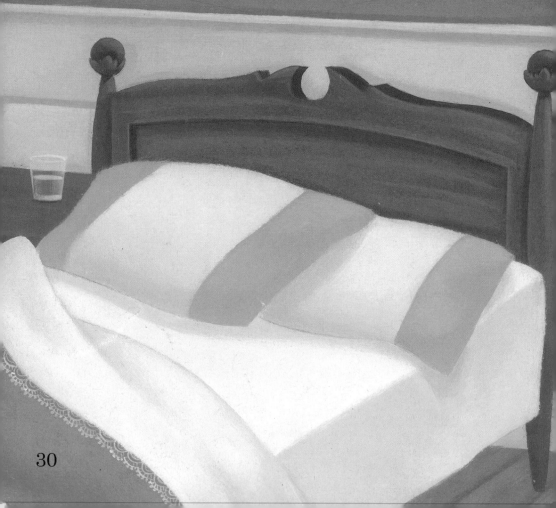

Clara's father was worried about Heidi. "I'll help you to go home," he said.

Heidi went to see Clara. "I will miss you when I am back in the mountains," she said.

"I will miss you, too," said Clara. "But I will come and see you one day soon."

So Heidi went back to the mountains. Grandfather and Peter were very happy to see her. Peter gave her some goats' milk. Then Heidi went to sleep in the hayloft.

Heidi didn't walk in her sleep that night. She was so happy to be home.

The next day, Heidi went to look after the goats with Peter.

"It's wonderful to have you back," said Peter. "I missed you."

"I missed you, too," said Heidi. "I want to stay in the mountains forever."

One morning, when Heidi had just got up, there was a knock at the door. It was Clara and her father.

"I have to go to town," said Clara's father. "Clara can stay here with you for a week."

Heidi was pleased to see Clara, and took her to see all the beautiful things in the mountains.

But Peter was jealous of Heidi's new friend. When no one was looking, he pushed Clara's wheelchair down the mountain.

The next day, Clara could not find her wheelchair.

"I must try to walk," said Clara. So Heidi and her grandfather helped her to walk.

Suddenly, Clara started to walk all by herself. "This is wonderful!" said Heidi.

Peter was pleased, too. "I'm so sorry I was jealous," said Peter. "Will you be my friend, Clara?"

The next day, Clara's father came to take her back home. Clara walked out of the house to meet him.

"You can walk!" said Clara's father. "This is the happiest day of my life."

And Heidi, Clara and Peter were friends forever.

How much do you remember about the story of Heidi? Answer these questions and find out!

- Who does Heidi live with in the town in Switzerland?

- Who looks after the goats in the mountains?

- What is the name of Heidi's favourite little white goat?

- Why does Heidi have to go to Frankfurt?

- What does Peter do to Clara's wheelchair?

- Why is Clara's father surprised at the end?

Unjumble these words to make words from the story, then match them to the correct pictures.

tomianuns   Hiied   natherdfarg

Preet   Swonlakfe   Craal

Read it yourself with Ladybird

Tick the books you've read!

For more confident readers who can read simple stories with help.

Level 3

 YOU won't like this present as much as I DO!

 The Elves and the Shoemaker ☑

 Hansel and Gretel ☐

 Harry and the Bucketful of Dinosaurs ☐

 Jack and the Beanstalk ☐

 Furi on Music Island ☐

 Poppet Stows Away ☐

 Rapunzel

 The Red Knight ☐

Longer stories for more independent, fluent readers.

Level 4

I am Inventing an INVENTION ☐

Harry and the Dinosaurs United ☐

Heidi ☑

Katsuma and the Art Thief ☐

Luvli and the Glump-a-tron ☐

The Pied Piper of Hamelin ☐

Sam and the Robots ☐

Snow White and the Seven Dwarfs ☐

The Wizard of Oz ☐